DATE DUE

JAMES STEVENSON

DON'T MAKE ME LAUGH

FRANCES FOSTER BOOKS
FARRAR, STRAUS AND GIROUX
NEW YORK

Distributed in Canada by Douglas & McIntyre Ltd.
Color separations by Hong Kong Scanner Arts
Printed and bound in the United States of America by Berryville Graphics
First edition, 1999
Third printing, 1999

Library of Congress Cataloging-in-Publication Data
Stevenson, James, 1929–
    Don't make me laugh / James Stevenson. — 1st ed.
        p.   cm.
    "Frances Foster books."
    Summary: Readers are requested not to laugh or do anything to influence the
behavior of various animal characters in this book.
    ISBN 0-374-31827-1
    [1. Laughter—Fiction.   2. Behavior—Fiction.   3. Animals—Fiction.]   I. Title.
PZ7.S8445Do   1999
[E]–dc21   98-41780

THE RULES

How do you do?
I am Mr. Frimdimpny.
I am in charge
of this book.

I make up the rules.
If you wish to
read this book, you
must follow the rules.
Here they are . . .

. . . Are you
LISTENING?

Rule number 1 says:
DO NOT LAUGH!

Rule number 2 says:
DO NOT EVEN SMILE.

If you laugh or smile,
you have to go back
to the front
of the book!

It's *that* way!

Personally, I never ever laugh
or smile.   Ever   ever

ever

ever

ever

ever

ever

ever . . .

Nothing could
possibly make me.

Maybe *you* should go
look in the mirror and
practice *not* smiling.

. . . I will wait here.

You're back?
Good.
There is one last rule:
**DON'T DO ANYTHING
YOU ARE TOLD
NOT TO DO!**

Now you may read the book.
But remember the rules!

I will be watching you!

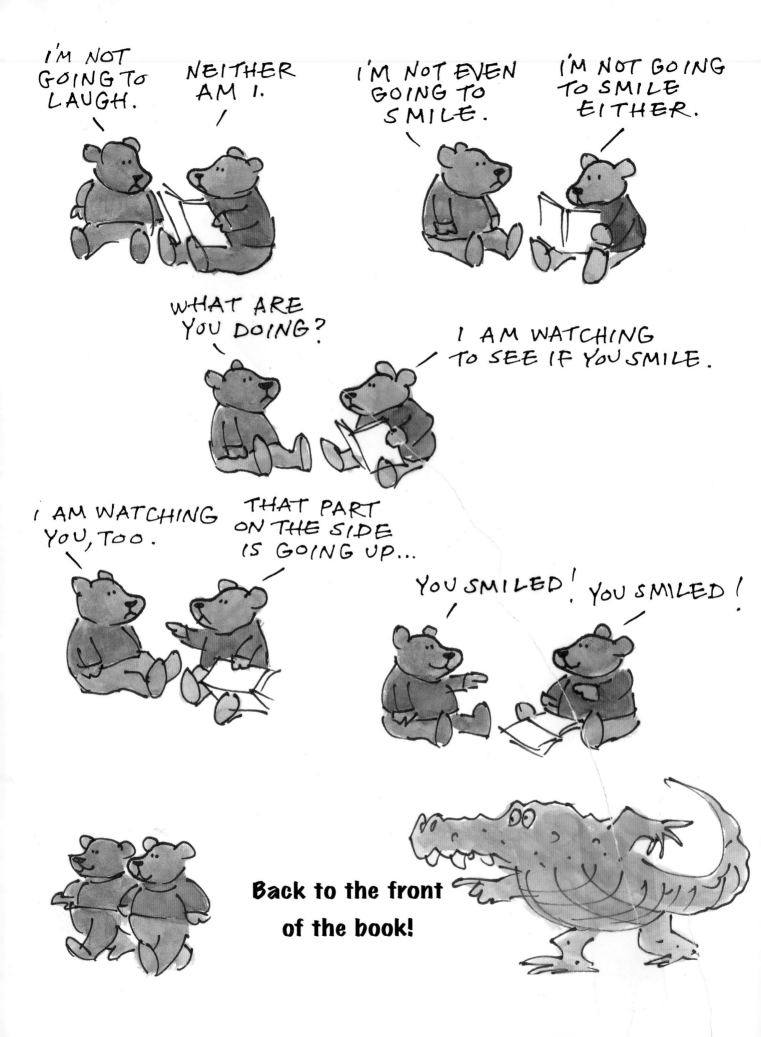

**Back to the front
of the book!**

PIERRE, THE EXCELLENT WAITER

I am Pierre, the excellent waiter.

I have but one request.
Please . . . do not
make me laugh.

I do not laugh often.
I laugh only if someone
tickles me in a certain spot.
I will mark that spot with a red X,
so no one will touch it by mistake.

Now I will pick up my enormous tray of food.

On my tray, I am carrying the soup, the spaghetti and meatballs, the green peas, the mashed potatoes, the large salad, the side order of slippery, slithery asparagus . . .

Wait . . . What are you looking at?

You are staring at my red X. What are you thinking?

OH, NO!

DON'T *DO* IT!

DON'T TOUCH THE X!

. . . It was a *simple* request.

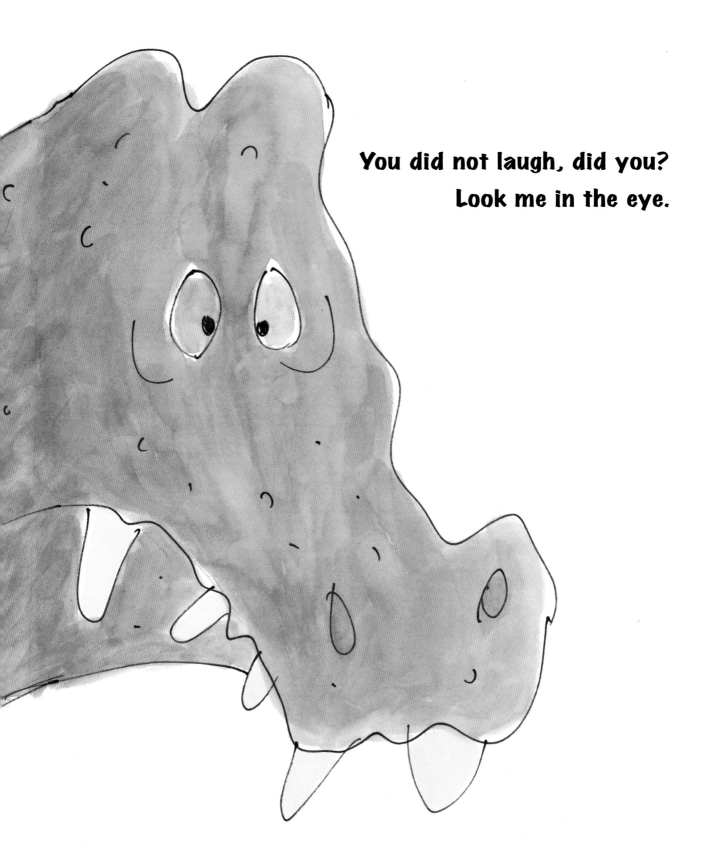

You did not laugh, did you?
Look me in the eye.

FENDENTLY'S TERRIBLE COLD

I have a terrible cold.

The slightest breeze could make me sneeze.

Please don't make me sneeze!

Do not make Fendently sneeze, whatever you do.

I feel you breathing.
Please stop.

Your breathing could make me sneeze.

Thank you for not breathing.

. . . Perhaps you would like to take
a breath now?

Please go far away to do it.

SHNOOF
SHNUF

Farther than that.

Even farther, please.

. . . A little farther . . .

Uh-oh . . .

Even from way over here . . .

I feel the breeze from your breathing . . .

KA---KA---KA---

KA---

OOF! Now look what you did!
Go back to the front of the book!

THE FANCY GLASS STORE

Hello! Welcome to the fancy
glass store! Look around all you like . . .

but do not sing, or whistle, or hum!

When I hear singing, whistling,
or humming, I cannot help myself . . .

I start to dance!

. . . Dancing is not a good thing to do
in a fancy glass store.

. . . So do not sing, whistle, or hum!

Thank you very much.

You heard what he said?
No singing!
No whistling!
No humming!

Oh . . . Oh . . .
What's that I hear?
Something like . . .
music?

. . . Now I must dance!
Here I go!

La-la-la! I'm dancing out the door
and down the street.

I heard you . . . You hummed!
. . . You whistled!
. . . You *sang*!

Go back
to the front
of the book!

THE TEST

I think . . . you
are smiling a
tiny bit . . . No?
We shall see
about that.
Help me conduct
a test, please.

Put your nose here

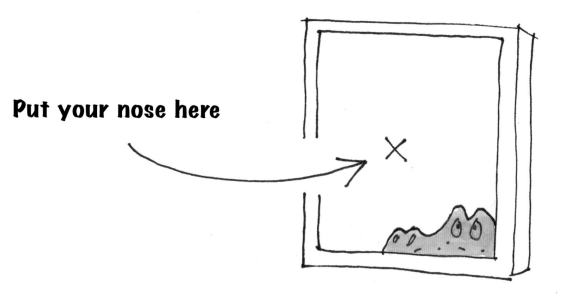

so I can get a good look at your face . . .

OH . . . YOUR FACE IS REALLY FUNNY!

In fact, I am starting
to . . . SMILE!

OH, NO!

Guess where I'm going!

THE FRONT
OF THE BOOK
IS <u>THAT</u> WAY !

The End